Renovating Christmas

A Skyline Mountain Novelette

LESIA FLYNN

This is a work of fiction. Names, characters, places, and
incidents are either the product of the author's imagination or
are used fictitiously, and any resemblance to actual persons,
living or dead, business establishments, events or locales is
entirely coincidental.

Renovating Christmas, Copyright 2014 by Lesia Flynn

Cover Art by Lesia Flynn with contributions by
Altafulla/Shutterstock and Mayovskyy Andrew/Shutterstock

ISBN-13: 978-0-9909908-3-3

ISBN-10: 0990990834

Select praise
from Amazon readers for
RENOVATING CHRISTMAS
by

LESIA FLYNN

"A wonderful story and I loved every word . . .
humor and romance in a story you can't put down
until you're finished!"
--NJZ

"It captured me from start to finish . . . smooth
reading and done before I knew it. Wanting more."
--PS

"Intelligent, witty, warm writing. . . Encore!"
--MJH

"A cute story that will keep you smiling."
--TA

"A fun entertaining quick read!"
--M

"A fun story, with zany characters."
--JS

For Chuck, my very own hero.

ACKNOWLEDGMENTS

My heartfelt thanks to Alicia Hunter Pace, Lynn Raye Harris, Bambi Lynn, Margie Burchfield, and Shelly Schoenfelder. Without you, there would be no first book.

Also, a big thank you to my girls whose encouragement keeps me going.

CHAPTER ONE

"JON, I CAN'T take this job."

"Why not? You're an electrician. Don't you get paid for hanging Christmas lights?"

Ben rolled his eyes at his old friend. "I do. But your Homeowner's Association Agreement says you have to do this personally, with friends and family at the most."

Jon Frazer sighed heavily. "How do you know?"

Ben pulled Jon aside into a man-to-man huddle. "Look man, folks have tried to hire me to hang lights here before. Mr. Dickerson, the Homeowner's Association President takes this thing seriously. I'm sure he's watching for electricians coming into the neighborhood. He's bound to have seen my truck already, so it's only a matter of time before he shows up. I'd help you out old friend, but I've got more paying jobs than I can keep up with. Just get one of the neighbors to help you put the lights out this year. It'll be a lot simpler, trust me."

"What in the Sam Hill is going on here, Ben?"

Jon Frazer, the new owner of 1225 Skyline Drive, turned with his old friend Ben to find the one and only Mr. Homeowners-Association-Thundercloud Dickerson marching headstrong towards them.

"I'm sorry, buddy." Fear swept across Ben's face. "Good luck finding some neighborly help!" He jumped in his truck, started the engine and took off like the fires of hell were after him, waving a frantic hand out of the side window as he drove away.

"Do tell me, Mr. Frazer. You were *not* attempting to hire an electrician to hang your Christmas lights, now were you?"

Mr. Dickerson wasn't exactly a looming bear of a man, but he carried authority like a cloak of dominance around his shoulders and boomed a mighty threat with his voice, as well.

Jon slumped to his side and reached up with one hand to squeeze the tension from his forehead. He fully expected to see a clipboard thrown in his face any second with more documents to read, maybe even copies of the ones he'd already signed when he closed the purchase just two days ago on the old house behind him. He knew he was going to regret the words, but he had to ask. Just maybe asking would get him back to work faster. "Why don't you refresh my memory on why I can't hire someone to hang my lights? It's Dickerson, right? Mr. Dickerson?"

Mr. Dickerson smiled wide with a hint of evil dripping to one side. "Dicker. Everyone calls me Dicker." And in a flash he had his smart phone up between them, showing the evidence of a homeowner's agreement for 1225 Skyline Drive situated on Skyline Mountain just above the small town of Riverland, Alabama. "If you had actually *read* the document you signed at the closing of your house, Mr. Frazer, you would know what the rules are for *Skyline Christmas*." He spat each word with disapproval then paused with what was quickly becoming a familiar evil smile. "Lucky for you I have that document right here." He pushed the device closer to Jon's face. "In fact, why don't I just shoot it over to you in an email so you can study it, *closely*?" Thrilled at the idea, he carried on with his phone until the task was complete. "Now I expect to see those lights out by Thanksgiving. *That's the rules,* Mister! You've got one week to get it done." And with a shooting motion of his hand imitating a gunshot and a weird popping sound from his mouth, Dicker spun on his heels and was off to invade someone else's world.

Jon crammed his hands into the back pockets of

his jeans and watched as the needling 'Dicker' marched away.

"He's really not so bad."

Surprised, Jon turned to find a woman just behind his right shoulder smiling up at him.

"Well, once you get used to the idea that he's always around." Her smile grew wider as she offered a hand to shake. "Hello."

Jon took her hand into his and instantly noted a multitude of differences between them. His hard, hers soft. His large, hers small. His . . .

"Welcome to the neighborhood." She grinned up at him and pulled her hand back to return it to the warmth of her pocket.

Jon could've sworn lights twinkled in her eyes with trills of laughter, whimsy and fun. And for some reason he knew instantly that he had an ally, a partner in crime, a friend. "Hi."

She laughed lightly and the warm air escaping her lips fogged in the cold November air. "I'm Christy. Christy Layne." She turned a quarter turn and pointed. "I live across the street at 1224."

Jon looked across the street, taking in the meticulous landscape, accentuated by lights that promised a display of fun and the childlike enthusiasm of the season. He'd seen Christy working on the lights in the dark the night before. He remembered she'd only lit them for the blink of an eye, probably to see what worked and what didn't. But in that quick preview he'd seen clearly that it was the home of young children anticipating the arrival of Christmas. A home. A family. Something special. A special something he himself longed for but hadn't realized until recently.

"You look a little shell-shocked at the idea of putting out lights." Still smiling she tilted her head, indicating that it wasn't a statement but a question.

Jon laughed halfheartedly. "You could say that. I've got three weeks to get the house ready to move in to before my lease is up. The last thing I need is to take on another task." He looked back at the house he'd acquired and felt the pull to get to work, returning the old house to its original glory.

"It's a beautiful old house. Surely there's not that much to do to ready it for your move?"

Jon turned back to face her. "I'm sorry. I didn't introduce myself." He fumbled with his wallet and pulled out his card. "I'm Jon Frazer, owner of Regenerations. I refurbish old structures to their original state and bring them up to code. Well, and current trends if it's possible to do so without compromising their history." He motioned at his house, "this place needs a lot of care right now. I wanted to get most of the interior, if not all of it, done before I move in."

Christy smiled up at him. Her eyes sparkled mischief as they locked in on his. "Then we have to get a move on, don't we?" She reached out and took his hand again. "Come on over and let's make a plan over some hot chocolate. Then Rudi and I can help you put it all together!" She gave him a tug. "Come on! What do you say?"

Jon glanced back at the house calling for him to repair her and gave in to the warmth and cheer of the woman pulling him along. *One thing at a time*, he told himself. *One thing at a time*.

CHAPTER TWO

CHRISTY POURED hot cocoa into large mugs at the breakfast table. She couldn't believe her good fortune to have the new homeowner from across the street sitting at her table. Even if it was a bit coerced. He was nice to look at yes, but even better was someone in the neighborhood in her own age bracket. Most folks around here were grandparents or beyond. Setting the pitcher of chocolate yum aside, she took a seat and pulled out a notebook. She opened it to a picture drawn on the page that perfectly matched her own yard and slid it over to Jon. "This is the plan I implement each year." She slid an inquisitive smile over at him. "Maybe we can make a similar plan for you so it's easy to navigate and assemble?"

Jon looked the drawing over. "Maybe I should read the rules before we put this in writing. He sighed, "I don't have any Christmas decorations." Worry crossed his face. "I'm just a bachelor. I've never had any reason to decorate for Christmas." He fumbled with the notebook. "This *Skyline Christmas* gig is a startup job for me."

Christy laughed then and touched his hand, pulling it away from the notebook into her own. "It's okay, Jon. It's really not so hard. Most of the required items are probably stowed away in your attic already. All you really have to have are some wreaths, garlands, candles, and lights." She gave his hand another squeeze of encouragement. "Well, and a fresh cut tree for the street and a personal item of choice." Again, her eyes lit up with something special. "Like my pair of lighted reindeer, Rudi's choice, of course. We just need to see what you have there and work on the personal touches."

Christy watched him consider what she said. He picked up his cup and drew in a long sip before setting it back on the table. Finally, he nodded and squeezed her hand in agreement. "So, the wreaths, garlands, candles, and lights are probably in the attic. That's easy enough, right?"

"Most likely, but I can't promise. Some folks around here are die-hards and insist on using live wreaths and such. But we'll look and see what you have and then make a shopping list, okay?"

Christy's phone rang and she checked to see who was calling. "I'm sorry. I've got to take this.

It's a client. Why don't you look over the homeowner documents while I take care of business for a minute. It'll put your mind at ease." She watched for his response as the phone continued to ring. He nodded in agreement and Christy answered her call by taking it into the office.

JON FOUND THE documents to be exactly as Dicker had said and of course, legally binding. The worst part of it were the fines for not participating, fifty bucks a day until compliance was met or a whopping twenty-five hundred for ignoring the season altogether! Surely he could take this on in its most simple fashion and pull it all together like Christy said he could.

He could hear Christy in the other room tap-tap-tapping on her keyboard and talking with someone, smoothing their feathers it sounded like. She seemed to be really good at that, the handling people's nerves part. She had a way about her that made him feel the stress around him fall away. She was a refreshing change in his life. He could get used to having a woman in his life that was kind and encouraging and enthusiastic about life. Most of the women he'd known in the past were only looking out for themselves and what they could get out of him.

He stood up and walked around the room taking in the tidy atmosphere and attention to detail. The room was simple, obviously not the original kitchen like his. He ran a hand across the edge of the stovetop. Late 1980s remodel, maybe? The room was clean, and despite its age, it had an eloquent quality that he was sure came from Christy. She had a flair for the arts it seemed. On the counter there was a set of colored glass canisters, a hand painted cake dome in bright colors that was filled with muffins, and an individual serving coffee machine. On the fridge was one single item, a child's drawing of a stick woman holding a stick girl's hand, the prominent part being the smiles on their faces. Written in the sky were the words, *I love you Momma*. A red heart followed the sentiment and it was signed, Rudi, age 8. Jon smiled. Christy was loved. And maybe single, he noted, by the looks of no male figure in the drawing.

Jon's phone beeped and interrupted his thoughts. A text from the local newsroom appeared, announcing fire trucks on the scene of what appeared to be an electrical fire started by faulty wires.

Jon frowned. He looked out through the window to see his new house; memories of an older house ablaze flickered in the back of his mind.

He could still feel the heat from the flames

devouring his childhood house as he and his
parents watched from the safety of the street. His
father pulled him into his side as the firefighters
worked their stations to battle the blaze. The noises.
The smells. The sobs of his mother's voice. It all hit
him square in the face, again. A firefighter
approached them when the house finally melted
down to a smolder. "Seems like the old electrical
wires are to blame." He sighed as he patted the
elder Frazer on the shoulder. "They'll know for
sure once the investigation is complete." That's
when Jon's father eased his big body away from the
little boy. Jon reached for his hand to pull him back.
"Stay." His eyes pleaded with his father. "Please
stay." But in the end, the man left carrying away
the shame of his inability to provide safety for his
family.

A mail truck stopped in front of 1225 Skyline
Drive and brought Jon back to the present. Nope.
His wiring had checked out just fine. He'd made
certain of that before making an offer on the old
house. He'd even had his old buddy Ben the
electrician go behind the inspector to verify that the
house had been rewired completely. Newing up
electrical wires wasn't something Jon was willing to
take on with this remodel. It was too time
consuming for the urgency he felt in this present
life-changing renovation. Something in him said
timing was of the essence and he was letting his gut

lead the way.

Relieved by his thoughts, Jon placed his phone on his belt and returned his eyes to the house across the way. He pictured the place in its refreshed state gleaming back at him, fresh paint, repaired gutters, a refurbished front door with its stained glass inlay gleaming the warmth of home and hearth from within. But for the life of him he couldn't get past the insistence of wreaths on all the windows. There they were right in the big middle of his imaginings, inhabiting all of the front face windows with red ribbons waving in the wind.

"Day-dreaming about what it will be?" Christy brought laughter back into the room with each step. She sidled up beside him and peered out in the same direction. "No worries, my friend. It's going to be beautiful!" She nodded with certainty.

Jon nodded back with a little less certainty, but he nodded just the same.

Christy set about cleaning up the cups of cocoa. "Let's go see if you have anything in the attic to work with before I need to get back to work, shall we? It won't take but a few minutes, and then we can both move forward with peace of mind."

Jon found himself spinning in her quick acting determination. He mulled it over for a second and made up his mind. There really wasn't any avoiding the issue because he wasn't about to get caught up in paying fines for the lack of Christmas

decorations! "All right. Let's go see what I've got."
He laughed softly. "We'll make a list and check it
twice."

Christy beamed back at him, eyes sparkling
bright. "There's hope for you yet, Jon Frazer!"

CHAPTER THREE

AFTER A THOROUGH assessment of the attic findings, it was agreed, the decorations were a bust. The ribbons were faded and torn, the artificial wreaths were weather worn and the lights, well, frankly Jon was afraid of the lights. They appeared to be the same age as the house. He couldn't bring himself to plug the vintage lights into a socket. And there wasn't a window candle to be seen anywhere. All of which was why he stood knee deep in the lights department at the local hardware store Friday after working on his new old house all day long. Christy and Rudi had promised to meet him to help gather the Christmas decoration essentials. Rudi had dubbed the mission *Operation Skyline Christmas*. The plan was to keep it simple. The only exception was Jon insisted on live greenery, not artificial because he wanted to keep with the Arts and Crafts era of the house.

So there he was in the hardware store, never having shopped for holiday lights before. There were so many different types. So many colors, too. Big lights, little lights, mini lights, LED lights, blinking lights, musically programmed lights? What? He was in way over his head and he knew it. Maybe the fine was worth it just this once so he could have a whole year to wrap his head around a Christmas lights project. Then he thought about the price tag of replacing the kitchen floor and shook off the idea.

He reached for one last box of lights to examine before giving up entirely and heard a familiar voice nearby. He knew that voice but he couldn't match it to a face. A sales clerk came around the corner to his right and then he remembered who the voice belonged to. But it was too late. Dicker spotted him and was in full thunder mode. He marched up to take the lead of the clerk and slammed his hands down on his hips, projecting all of his portly five and a half feet of authority toward Jon, demanding a plan of action without even saying a word.

"Well? What's it going to be Mr. Frazer?" He sneered and his beady little eyes accused Jon to the depths of his soul. "Your cart is empty. Are you going to man up and abide by the contract or am I going to have to fine you?" He rubbed his greedy little hands together as if caressing the dollar bills he already thought were coming his way. "We'll be happy to let you fund the reconstruction of our neighborhood swimming pool. It's in *great* disrepair."

Jon sighed. "Look, Mr. Dickerson."

Dicker waved a short, beefy finger at him. "Uhuhuh, now. Name's Dicker to my friends and neighbors."

"Dicker." Jon ran a hand across his face, producing a scratching sound. He was tired. The day had begun with renewed excitement to make repairs only to be interrupted by Dicker, who of course left a storm cloud of bad events in his wake. Jon had busted an antique stained glass window and followed that up by putting a dent in his truck, not to mention he had achieved nothing on the new house, save the broken window. This day was off track and he was taking it back under control. "Like I said this morning, Dicker, I've got every intention of doing right by my word. You're going to have to back off and give me the time and space to make it happen, all right? I don't need you hovering like a mother hen."

Just as the word 'hovering' left Jon's lips, Christy rounded the corner with a cart loaded heavily with fresh wreaths, ribbons, candles and a garland. Rudi wasn't far behind.

Jon looked to the sky and offered up a silent

prayer of thanks for the little rescue. Dicker spit and sputtered some nonsense about backing off when he was good and ready at a volume half the store could hear.

Christy smiled broadly at Jon and winked. "Hello Dicker. What a pleasant surprise! I didn't expect to see *you* here tonight."

Dicker deflated as fast as he'd been enraged when Christy patted his arm like they were best buddies.

"Hi Mr. Dick!" Rudi piped up as she rounded her mother.

Dicker's face exploded in a rage of red. "My name is Dicker, not Dick and not Mr. Dick. Just Dicker." He turned to find Christy holding a hand over her mouth, obviously attempting to hide the laughter. "Christy for the love of God will you ever get control of your child?"

Rudi pulled on his shirt sleeve. "Are you here to buy *more* lights for your yard?" Her eyes got big as saucers. "Didn't the Fire Marshall tell you last year not to add anything else or your house might burn down?"

Dicker looked at each one individually, threw up his hands, and sputtered something under his breath as he turned and marched out faster than he'd entered.

The sales clerk ran a safe distance in the opposite direction.

Christy bent over in laughter.

"I think that man's stalking me."

Christy stood with her arms wrapped around her middle, trying to control the laughter. The whole scene was completely lost on Rudi so she skipped away and began examining snow globes displayed on the end cap.

"Is he like this with everyone in the neighborhood?"

"I'm afraid so." Christy tried deep breaths to ward off another round of laughing.

"Geesh! The man's a little over the top, don't you think? You know, he rang my doorbell at six this morning?"

Christy finally sighed and wiped her tears away as she gathered herself. "Well, he's been bored lately. It's been a while since anyone new moved in, and it being Christmastime, well." She raised her hands and lifted her shoulders in question. "Let's just say you're getting a concentrated dose of Dicker." She sniffed and wiped an errant tear. "Don't take him so seriously, he's harmless most of the time. Believe me." She rolled her eyes. "I know all too well just how pesky he can be."

"Yeah? Why is that?"

Christy shrugged as she responded. "He's my landlord. I've had to learn how to interact with him without losing my cool." She smiled. "You just have to learn how to work around him and not push his buttons."

"If you say so." Jon shook his head.

"You probably don't want to tell him to back off next go around. It's a sure way to set him off."

"Next time?" Jon looked horrified. "Does there have to be a next time?"

Christy giggled. "Oh. There's always a next time. And try not to make a habit of calling him Mr. Dick, either."

They laughed together then. "You've got some kid there, Christy. She's all right!"

Christy beamed with pride. "Thank you, Jon. That's the sweetest thing anyone's ever said to me."

Jon saw that light in her again as he watched her response. Then he did something he hadn't done in a very long time. He decided right there that a girl, this girl Christy Layne, was all right too.

"Come on you guys!" Rudi grabbed her mother's hand and pulled. The big lights are over on the other side."

And making a quick escape several hundred dollars later, the three of them set off for a little Christmas fun.

CHAPTER FOUR

JON CONCENTRATED on sketching out the light details while Christy put Rudi to bed for the night. The three of them had spent the last two hours hanging greenery outside and cleaning interior windowsills to place the candle lights inside. Jon learned that Rudi would do just about anything when fueled by hot chocolate, so the stuff ran full tilt and she cleaned like a pro. The problem was, eventually there was a meltdown and Rudi had to recharge her batteries the healthy way, sleep.

A soft knock sounded on the old front door. Christy let herself in before Jon could get up from a chair left in the room by the previous owner. She stopped in the entry and smiled, then pushed a strand of hair behind her ear.

"All's well in dreamland?"

Christy nodded. "She was out before her feet

were off the ground." She sighed. "I had to boost her up into the blankets myself." She tugged on the arms of her sweater and wrapped herself tight. "I believe it's getting a little chilly outside." She shivered.

"It's about time, don't you think? We should've been in full thermal gear at least a few weeks ago."

She laughed. "I was starting to think Thanksgiving was going to be warm and our reveal night would need cold chocolate milk and cookies instead of hot cocoa."

Jon laughed. "I take it you're one of those that prays for snow in the south every year?"

Christy's face lit up and exposed her inner youthfulness. "Oh yes!" she exclaimed. "If I had my way it would snow for Thanksgiving, Christmas, New Year's, and Valentine's Day, too!"

Jon felt his heart kick at the excitement she exhibited. She made him feel things he hadn't believed possible, things maybe he had given up on ever finding for himself. He shook the notion off and noted it. He would think about his feelings later when he was alone.

"What have you got there?" Christy pointed to the notebook in Jon's lap.

"Oh, I picked up a notebook like yours to make the light plan, just as you suggested." He pushed the foot of the worn recliner down and motioned her further into the room. "Take a look and see if what I've got figured out works, will you?"

Christy went to his side and leaned over his shoulder to see the drawing of the lights and such laid out. Her hair slipped in front of her shoulders and the sweet scent tickled Jon's nose. She was close enough that he wrapped an arm around her and pulled her in closer, which got her attention. And for the first time since they'd met he looked into her eyes beyond the sparks of laughter and viewed the woman looking back at him. A woman full of love, and care, and passion for life. Christy looked at him then, her eyes open, and Jon saw her vulnerabilities and her inner secrets. He watched as a flash of hunger crossed her eyes, just enough to know he wasn't the only one feeling something between them. And before he could stop himself, he pulled her in and let his lips lightly touch hers, testing to make sure he was reading her right. She sighed. And just that little sound urged him to reach under, scoop her up behind her knees, and pull her into his lap.

Christy broke the kiss with nervous laughter. She pulled back a little and touched his lips with her fingertip. "What are we doing here, Jon?" She nudged his nose gently with her own and he took another taste of her lips.

"Kissing." He slipped a hand just under the hem of her sweater at the small of her back to feel her soft, warm skin.

Again she pulled away but kept herself nose to nose with him while she touched his face. "Hmm. Rudi would say we were tasting each other."

Jon turned just enough to snag an errant finger between his lips and caught her in his sight. "Hmm. Rudi would be right." He held her with his eyes and let some of himself open to her gaze as his fingers continued to suggestively dance across her skin. His eyes dipped down to take in her wet lips. "I like the way you taste, Christy." He swiped his tongue across her bottom lip. "I like the way you taste, a lot." And then he took her mouth, invaded her senses, and pulled her into him.

The lights dimmed in that way they do when there's an electrical storm threatening to black out the night, startling Jon. He broke the kiss and looked around his unfamiliar house. "That couldn't have been good." He lifted his senses and checked the air for signs of electrical smoke. "I don't smell anything, do you?"

Christy smiled easily. "Oh, it's nothing to worry about."

"No? Why's that?"

"We all get these little surges in the neighborhood when Dicker checks his lights at night." She laughed again and pushed to get up. "He always checks them at the same time every night just before he goes to bed. Like maybe they'll stop working or something. The testing usually begins at the first of November. His lights are all out by Halloween night." She laughed, backing away from him. "I don't think anyone's ever told him what happens, but we all know." She shook her head. "Oh, and he drains the system every year. You need to know that."

"I'm guessing that's why the Fire Marshall made last year's visit?"

Christy grabbed Jon's hand and tugged hard. "Come on! Quick! Let's go see what he's got going on." A mischievous grin lit up her face as she pulled him to the door.

"What about Rudi?"

"Oh. She's fine. It's only two houses down on the street beside my house and she knows I go look when I can. She'll be fine, I promise!" Christy tugged again to get him moving. "Besides, she's sound asleep." She rolled her eyes at him. "Somebody I know tanked her up on sugar all night!"

Her laughter filled his ears. How could he refuse to follow, even if it did pull her out of his arms?

THEY JOGGED AROUND the corner of the block to find Dicker's house in full Christmas regalia. The run was a good cover for the thunder of her heart that ensued from Jon's kisses. Geesh, but he'd taken her by surprise. What else could she do but use the lights as an escape? And *Holy Cannoli!* What an escape! Dicker had outdone himself this time. He had every cartoon character known to man lighting up the night, maybe even a few that this generation had never heard of. Christy stopped in her tracks. Jon ran into her back and gazed at the glow emanating from Dicker's property, in shock, no doubt. Christy turned her head to see his face and chuckled at his surprise. "This is Dicker's thing. He likes to go one better than everyone else."

Jon shook his head. "I'm amazed he could pull that off! Wow." He made a coughing sound. "Just wow."

"Yeah. It's pretty out there. He changes it out every year. I can't imagine where he stores it all!"

"And what's with the inflatable turkey under that spotlight next door?"

Christy laughed. "Pure rebellion!"

"Why's that?'

Christy held a finger over her lips and made a shushing sound of conspiracy. "Because they can turn their spotlights on before Thanksgiving night!" She turned her head back around to take it all in again.

Jon slid his arms around her, pulled her back against his chest looping them together. They watched as the whole display twinkled, the music invaded the air, and a famous mouse danced with a reindeer on top of the roof.

"I think he has way too much time on his hands." Christy leaned in for more of the heat coming off Jon's body and shivered.

"Are you cold?" He pulled her tighter and nuzzled in next to her ear.

Christy, unable to help herself, leaned into his affections. It had been too long since she felt anything for a man. This was good. It felt right even though they had only just met. The thought of another Christmas alone had pressed on her for weeks now. Holidays were meant for family, fun, and thankfulness. Though she was thankful that she had Rudi, she felt emptier each year that passed since her young husband gave his life in the Middle East. Maybe this year would be different. Better. Happier.

"The roofline lights can't be easy to hang for some of these folks around here." Jon interrupted her thoughts. "It seems dangerous, even."

"It's been an issue at the Homeowners' meetings for a while now. Dicker's the only one holding the line on the "all decorations must be personally installed" requirement in the rules. Everyone else is on board to make changes."

"What is he thinking?" Jon shook his head in disbelief. "Is he holding out until someone gets hurt?"

Christy held up her hands in defense. "No need to convince me, Jon. I want it changed as much as anyone else around here, and I've got young legs. Most don't.

The night suddenly went black as ink and Dicker's nightly show was gone leaving the neighbor's turkey to wobble in the wind alone. Neither Jon nor Christy moved to turn back towards home. Christy listened to the night sounds and watched as a star twinkled up above. For some reason she wanted to record this very moment forever in her mind. It was important to remember this. Just this. This man and his warmth, his hold on her, his attention.

Jon nestled her ear. "You're awfully quiet all of a sudden."

"Mmm. I'm recording the moment."

"What? Like for a memory?"

She leaned her head back further into his heat and smiled as he kissed her neck. "I think this is an important moment in time. I just want to remember it."

He leaned away from her then. "What, like I'm going to go away or something?"

She turned to face him. "No. It's not like that. Besides, we barely know each other. I was just enjoying the moment and wanted to remember it, okay." She slid her eyes to meet his. What was that in his eyes? Hope? Longing? She tilted her head. "Is that okay that I would want to remember you holding me in the night?"

Jon didn't say anything. She couldn't read him. But he did lean in and touch her lips again.

Christy opened up to take as much as he would give. Because no one knew like she did how precious each moment was.

CHAPTER FIVE

TWO DAYS LATER, Christy launched the website for her latest client. She basked in the moment, enjoying the pride she felt for a job well done. She'd worked hard at designing the best pages she could for her clients, mostly authors and children's book illustrators. Starting out, she taught herself programming languages and design tools to catch up with the rest of the techy world while her belly rounded and later her baby Rudi cooed and crawled around her feet. Her drive to learn had served her well, especially when she found herself alone with a small child to raise. Though her warrior husband had left her with a hefty sum of life insurance, she never felt right about using any of it. What was left after the necessary funeral arrangements and such, was all lumped into a savings account for their baby girl to use for college or whatever life presented down the road. Christy figured she herself was young, healthy, and capable of taking care of her own life. So she did just that. She continued to learn and challenge herself to grow her business and provide as best she could for her little family.

Christy leaned back in her chair to stretch and glanced out of her office window. There on the other side of the street she saw Jon sporting a low hung tool belt on his long and lean body. He appeared to be busy unloading a window out of the bed of his truck. She looked at the clock on her computer screen. Thirty minutes until the school bus deposited Rudi at her doorstep. She glanced back towards 1225 Skyline Drive, enjoyed the view for just a few seconds longer. *Maybe she had lost herself in providing for Rudi for too long. Was it time to consider her own life again? Her own needs?* Jon stopped what he was doing and stood still with hand to hip. Curiosity got the best of her. She wrapped a scarf around her neck and slid into her winter coat to investigate the window and the man.

"Hey there stranger."

Jon looked up from the tailgate and his smile grew wide at the sight of her. He turned, leaving his project behind and sat back on the tailgate, letting his long legs stretch out in front of him. He hung his thumbs from the pockets of his jeans looking like a perfect picture of man-in-control.

Lordy, but the sight of him was enough to make her melt, Christy thought as she drank him in with her eyes.

"Hey there beautiful." His eyes lit up as he suggestively took in her appearance. "I haven't seen you for a few days. I was starting to think I might have to perform a rescue over there." He nodded toward her house as he reached a hand out to her.

Christy knew if she took his hand she'd be in his arms within seconds. Despite acknowledging how precious time was in the heat of the moment the other night in front of Dicker's light display, she'd been holding back, avoiding him. But the sight of him working in the sunshine drew her out. She locked eyes with him and threw in the towel, reaching out to accept his invitation. As sure as the winds got colder each day, Jon pulled her into him and kissed the thoughts right out of her brain. The only thing left inside her was the feeling of warmth and longing, hunger and promise. On a breathless sigh, she moved to nestle into his neck as he slipped his lips past her cheek.

"You taste like another." He nipped at her ear.

Christy laughed out loud and wiggled backwards to see his eyes. "What did you just say?"

Jon scooped her face into his big hands and met her nose to nose, smile to smile. "You taste like another. Haven't you ever heard that before?"

Christy shook her head, still amused.

"My mother used to say that when she found something tasty that she liked, usually a flavor of ice cream that had black walnuts in it." He leaned back and ran his thumbs across her cheeks. "You're the only thing I've ever found that tastes like another." He grinned.

"What? Don't you like black walnuts?" she teased.

He shook his head and barked with laughter. "Nope. I like the taste of you."

Christy snickered at the sight of him. Such a man, yet so boyishly playful. "Who are you, Jon Frazer?"

He tilted his head to question her. "What do you mean?"

She ran her hands down his chest and around to his sides and held him there, giving him a little shake. "Oh you're just so manly and yet here you are showing me the little boy inside you." She grinned at him tenderly.

He lifted an eyebrow in question. "Oh! You think I'm a boy, huh?" He grabbed her then, laughing, and hauled her over his shoulder fireman style and began walking towards the front door of the house like he had all the time in the world.

Christy squealed, slapping at his back playfully. "You put me down Jon Frazer! Giggles erupted making her wiggle and writhe on him. "Put me down! You're going to hurt yourself like this!"

Jon made it through the door and let her slide down the front of him, slow as you please, until her feet hit the floor. "Looks like I need to show you the man I am."

Christy let the laughter go as she caught the note in his voice and looked up. Before she could stop him he was fully involved with her mouth, pulling her up against his hard body and letting her feel just how much of a man he really was. She pushed back enough to say his name out loud and he took full advantage of realigning himself in a different angle to take her deeper.

"I haven't had a sound thought or a decent night's sleep in two days for thinking of you."

Christy gulped in air as he spoke, moaned when he slipped a hand up and under her breast to weigh, to feel, to squeeze. Her head fell backwards in surrender.

"God Christy. You are so beautiful. I want to move my mouth all over you. I want to taste all of you."

Christy sucked in a breath as he provoked a nipple.

Jon pulled her into another dance with his mouth.

Then the doorbell rang.

Christy jumped and pushed at him in alarm.

Jon cursed. "My bet it's Dicker." He ran the

back of his hand over his mouth and reached for the heavy wood door. But before opening it, he turned, looked back at her, and demanded her attention. "Save my place."

It wasn't a question. It was a command. Christy's girl parts turned to goo, her heart heaved a sigh, and then the door opened.

"This better be good old man."

"Hi Mr. Frazer. Have you seen my momma?"

Every ounce of blood drained from Christy's face and she froze, glued to the entryway floor as her child busted her in the arms of a man she barely knew.

Jon looked over his shoulder to check with Christy before speaking. He gave her a nod. She mimicked him stiffly giving the go-ahead. "Sure have. She and I were just going over *Operation Skyline Christmas.*"

Christy came to her senses and pushed around Jon to pull Rudi into a hug. "What are you doing here so early? It can't be that late." She poked her head through the door looking for the rear lights of the bus. Just how long had Jon Frazer wrapped her up in his sensual onslaught of delight?

"Mom! I get home every day at the same time. It's three fifteen, silly!" She made the universal gesture for crazy by swirling her fingers around her ears.

"Did you go to the house before you came over

here?"

"Sure. I dropped my backpack in my room then came looking for you. I figured you were over here kissing or something."

Christy stilled, her eyes got big. Her baby was onto her? What was she thinking? Of course Rudi was onto her. She was smart. Not to mention the fact that they had spent the past eight years together day in and day out. No one else knew her so well. Still, she was mortified and the red creeping up her neck was a sure sign of it, too.

Jon chuckled. "So, smarty-pants. Are you okay with me and your mom kissing or should I go far, far away?"

Rudi looked up at Jon, snickered and replied, "Sure! So long as kissing doesn't make you throw up. I personally think it's gross!" She stuck her tongue out, bent slightly and faked a gag to express her undeniable repulsion of such things.

Jon threw his head back and let out a bark of laughter, making the sound echo throughout the empty rooms. "You're all right, Rudi." He threw an arm around her small frame and headed down the hall. "Come on. Let's go find us something warm to drink before we put out the spotlights."

Rudi skipped a step or two. "Oooh! Yummy! Do you have any more hot chocolate?"

"No hot chocolate today!" Christy threw out at their backs. "Zilch! Nada! None!"

Rudi and Jon slumped, but they continued forward while Christy tried to wrap her head around what had just happened.

CHAPTER SIX

OPERATION SKYLINE CHRISTMAS wasn't going as simply as Jon had imagined. Oh, the lights were all out just fine. The wreaths and candles, too. But that one personal element he was required to display had not come with appreciation from Dicker. Of course, Dicker was quite verbal about it.

"You cannot call a garden gnome a Christmas decoration!"

Jon remembered how good it felt to let his face stretch in delight over that little incident. "Why not?" he said. "It's got a red hat and a green coat, and it's a personal lawn ornament. And besides that, I put some white lights around his feet like he's standing in snow."

Jon had laughed so hard in the wake of Dicker's exit that he thought he saw a neighbor or two peeking out of their windows to see the commotion. And he gave a thought of appreciation to Rudi for thinking of the snow detail.

In the moment, all he really had left on the lights display was posting a tree at the street and stringing the lights on it. All easy enough, true. But like Dicker, Jon wasn't feeling the personal element in the grand scheme of his display. He knew there was something missing, but it hadn't revealed itself to him just yet. It was niggling at him in the back of his mind, though. And Jon knew he'd have to act quickly when the time came.

But in the meantime, the house project was the one being neglected. He hadn't gotten the kitchen floor replaced per his self-imposed timeline, nor had he rebuilt the back door steps. But he had gotten a call from Bolton, a general contractor he worked with regularly who had come upon some wood flooring being pulled from a tear down. Bolton wanted to know if Jon wanted it before he called anyone else. And that had been consolation enough for him to let go of the pressure to get the kitchen floor job done. He now had in his possession enough aged hardwood flooring to add to his house like what was original to the building.

So his timeline was off, but given the new developments, he let it go. Besides, once *Skyline Christmas* opened on Thanksgiving night, he would have two more weeks to get the heavy stripping and sanding, the real dust producing jobs, out of the way. Then he could at least inhabit the house and evacuate his apartment located at the base of the mountain in Riverland.

He lifted his hand to knock on the door of 1224 Skyline, but before he could finish the task, the door swung open and Rudi welcomed him with joy, jumping up and down.

"I didn't think school was ever going to end today! Can we go get the trees now? Please?"

Christy walked up behind Rudi and beamed her enthusiasm along with Rudi. "Honey, be still and let him come inside out of the cold." Jon stepped forward and reached for Christy over Rudi's head and kissed her.

"Ew! Bleck!" Rudi took off into the living room to escape them.

Jon smiled into Christy, breathed her in a little longer. "I guess I know how to get you alone now."

Christy slid her hands around his waist and hugged tightly.

Jon held her there, relishing the feel of her against his body. "I'm hungry." Heat emanated off him in waves to let her know that, though it was dinnertime, he was not interested in food, but he wanted a lot more than a taste of her.

Christy nodded as she looked up at him and a knowing passed between them.

Jon pulled her back into his arms, letting her head rest against his chest. "Hey kiddo, are you hungry?"

Rudi bounded back at them. "Can we get burgers and milkshakes on the way? Please?"

Laughter erupted and cheers went up before Jon piled them all into his truck. The evening was looking up. And so it was, Jon pushed through the next few hours quickly so he could get a real taste of Christy Layne.

ONCE THE TREES were set and the lights completed, the temperature dropped swiftly and the nightly hour of Dicker's testing came and went. Since there was no school the next day, Christy decided to let Rudi stay up late and they all went for a walk to see the rest of the neighborhood's "test" display. It was a tradition set after everyone realized what Dicker's bedtime was and they all flipped their switches in unison and let lights blink and shine through the night for fifteen minutes or so the last few nights before the big event. Jon, Christy, and Rudi passed by the neighborhood park and saw that Santa's reindeer area was ready and waiting. Someone had lined the trees with white twinkling lights giving it the appearance of a winter wonderland. The night sky was deep in its darkness, offering the cold night its starlight from above. The wind bit into them as they walked.

"Someone else openly rebels against Dicker." Jon pointed to the cutout of a pair of pilgrim children praying in a yard to the right.

Christy laughed in agreement and shivered in the cold.

"Your nose is starting to look like Rudolf's," Jon exclaimed. He reached out and held his palm over her nose to warm it.

Christy's eyes got big. "I know. It's really getting cold out here." She looked up into the heavens, hoping, praying. "Maybe it'll snow!" She sighed.

"You're wasting your breath there, sweetheart. The weatherman says the likelihood is pretty slim to none."

"Yes, well he's been known to be wrong," she pouted. "Look over there at Julia's house," she pointed and smiled. "She still has her jack-o-lanterns lit from Halloween."

Jon howled with laughter. "Another defiant neighbor."

Christy laughed along with him. "She's another new homebuyer. She caught onto Dicker's bossiness and kicked back fast. She only just moved in at the end of summer before the school year started, I think. She teaches at Rudi's school."

Rudi sat down on the sidewalk ahead of them and stroked the back of someone's cat.

"Don't look now but I think the troops are

wearing out."

Jon tugged on her hand, pulling her around to face him. He reached in and touched her lips with his own. "I'm not ready to let you go tonight. Any chance I could wrangle more time out of you after she goes to sleep?"

Christy felt her heart flutter. Could it be that he wanted her? "What did you have in mind?" she cooed as she nipped at his lower lip.

A groan rumbled out of Jon as he pulled her tight against his body. "You're tempting the devil out of me, Christy." He pushed his way around and looked deep into her eyes. "I want you. All of you."

Christy watched his eyes grow dark and his nose flared in hunger. There was no mistaking the man. He reached up and held her face, gently stroking her cheek. Christy looked on, trying to decide what to say, what to do. *Could she finally let someone else into her life?* Jon ran his thumb across her lips. Christy watched the movement of his eyes follow the motion.

"Tell me no and I'll back off. But I do want you, Christy." His eyes moved back to hers, waiting for an answer.

Inside, she knew if she leaned into him, it would be all he needed to take that as a yes. Hadn't she waited long enough to risk her heart again? Hadn't she grieved and let her heart heal? Was she ready to accept a man in her life again? She looked at him and saw strength and beauty, integrity and kindness. He was everything she'd wanted more of in her life for a long time now. He could be a new beginning. And though he wasn't making any promises beyond tonight, she knew "beginning" was a step in the direction she wanted to go.

She leaned into him. "I want you too, Jon."

Rudi squeezed between them at that precise moment, insisting they break it up. "Momma, I'm too tired to walk home. Can you carry me?"

Jon reached over the child and placed his forehead to Christy. She felt his breath whisper across her lips. He gently kissed her, offering promises of more to come. Pulling away, he reached down and scooped a sleepy little girl up onto his shoulders, jumping slightly to position her safely there. "Can you hold on a little longer, Rudi?" He plied her hands from their grasp on his head. "Hold my hands tight and I'll get you home as fast as I can, okay baby?"

Christy's heart squeezed as Jon spoke the term of endearment to her little girl. It was the moment he took possession of her heart. One she locked into her memory, again. And as they turned around to head home, she gave herself permission to wish for Jon Frazer to be someone she could love for many Christmases to come.

CHAPTER SEVEN

JON WOKE UP to howling winds beating against the windows, the night's darkness still blanketed the wee hours of morning. Christy's body draped across the top of him, limp. He was satisfied like no other time in his life. He ran a hand softly over her hair. For months, he had felt restless, like his purpose in life had taken a wrong turn. That's why he had decided to buy a house for himself. He had spent too many years now doing just that for others, restoring their homes, renewing their lives. It was long overdue in his own life and he needed roots. He needed purpose. He needed a home.

Christy stirred and slipped a leg against his as if to confirm he was still there.

He held his breath, waiting for her to settle. And when she reached in her sleep for his hand and tucked it into her breast, he knew. Something about the way she moved cleared the veil of his heart so that he could see clearly the vision he had traveled these past months to find. He had traveled straight to her. *She* was his purpose. *She* was his home.

He smiled into the darkness before looking back to the windows where the chill of winter loomed. And though the winds continued to howl their cold despair, inside Jon finally felt a sense of calm, a comfort of warmth in his discovery of love. And though he wanted to stay right where he was, the day pulled at him to get started.

He eased out from under Christy, pulled on his jeans and quietly padded toward the hallway bathroom, thankful Christy had left the bathroom light on for the night. He was careful not to make a sound that would wake either Christy or Rudi. Of course, as life would have it, just as he placed a hand on the doorknob to push it open, Rudi pulled from the other side to catch him off guard, lights blaring straight to his brain cells. They both sucked in a breath of alarm. Jon shielded his eyes.

"Rudi! You scared the daylights out of me!" Jon placed his other hand over his heart as it thundered from his chest.

Rudi stared at him, appearing to let her sleepy mind catch up. "Hi Jon." Then she pushed past him and tippy-toed towards her own room.

Jon watched, wondering if he should give an explanation of why he was there. He did *not* have a clue, having never been in such a predicament before.

To his rescue, just before disappearing behind her own walls, Rudi turned and looked at him watching her. "Jon?" Her little girl voice gave a quiet sound in the night, one younger, more delicate than the daytime allowed.

"Rudi?"

"Are you going to stay with my momma? Always?"

Jon saw concern drape across her little girl shoulders. Her words hit him in the gut like a truck. And he knew. It had never been about a house, or the fire, or any faulty electrical wires. It had always been about family. About safety together. About staying. Years of uncertainty and pain fell off his shoulders. "Yes, Rudi. I want to stay with her. That is, if she'll be mine." He ran a nervous hand through his sleep-mussed hair. "Is that okay with you?"

Rudi nodded softly. "I'd like that." She sighed and let her small frame relax. "I think I'd like that very much." She wiped at her sleepy eyes. "I'm going back to sleep now."

Realization hit Jon as he looked on. He knew exactly what turn the day just took, one filled with a last minute *Skyline Christmas* project.

Rudi's door creaked as she began to close it. "Rudi?"

She poked her head out the door at Jon's voice.

"Can we keep this a secret, our little talk here? I'd like to make it a surprise for your mom."

A yawn filled her face. "Sure Jon. Good night."

RUDI STOOD AT the kitchen sink later that morning, peeling potatoes and singing her heart out to some ageless chipmunk holiday music. The smells of a feast were in the air as Christy stirred things on the stove preparing for the next day's festivities. Jon looked on with wonder and pride.

"The winds got pretty rough last night. I was thinking I'd walk the neighborhood and see if everyone's lights are still intact. If not, I could lend a hand to make repairs." He leaned over her shoulder to see what was sizzling in the pan. "What do you think? Is that a good idea?"

Christy turned her head and kissed his cheek. Pointing her wooden spoon at him she teased, "Careful there. You might find your name on the next Homeowners Association Officer's ballot!"

Jon grinned back and slipped his hands around her waist. "So long as I get to keep you, I'm up to it." He nipped at her ear.

"Hey! Stop that funny business! There's a kid in the room, you know!" Rudi rolled her laughing eyes at them and went back to singing, loudly, to drown out their presence.

Christy laughed out loud as Jon moved in closer and whispered, "If she only knew."

His phone beeped, stealing his attention away. "Hey, I've got to get this, okay?" He looked up to her eyes, waiting for her response, hoping he wasn't as transparent as he felt at the moment.

"Sure. Go." She moved her spoon in the air like a grand conductor. "I've got my hands full here."

He kissed her nose. "I'll check in with you later, okay. This phone call, then I'm off to check the neighborhood."

Jon hit "dial" as soon as he was outside, far enough away that there was no possibility of the girls overhearing his plans. On the second ring he heard just who he needed for a last minute change in plans. "Bear, my man! I need your help. Can you squeeze an emergency job in for me today?" He waited for a response, nodded his head, and gave a pump of victory with his arm to the air. He spelled out the details and ended the call after promising to make it up to his friend. As he walked the streets of his new neighborhood, checking in with the people and their decorations, Jon felt for the first time in a very long time that all was right in his world.

AFTER SECURING THE lights at several

houses and helping Julia dispose of her jack-o-lanterns, Jon checked in on Christy and Rudi before heading to Bear's to work on his "emergency job". He didn't know how he had landed this incredible opportunity with Christy, but the promises she whispered in his ear the night before were enough to urge him to finish the task and get back to her as soon as possible. Which he did, after one last stop along the way for a secret touch of sparkle for the *Operation Skyline Christmas* reveal.

Christy and Rudi were curled up together, watching as the local weatherman dashed all their hopes of a Thanksgiving snowfall when Jon slipped through the front door. The house smelled of a turkey baking and all the fixings waiting to go along side. Jon rubbed his belly, remembering just then that he'd been so busy, so excitedly busy, that he had completely forgotten about lunch. He eased himself down next to Christy and put his arm around her shoulders, effectively pulling her in tight. Rudi slid in for the huddle, too.

"Hey you! You've been a busy man today, haven't you?" Christy smiled up at him, searching his features, his expression.

"Yes I have." Jon beamed right back at her. "But it was a good day. A very good day."

"Hmm. I think you've got secrets, Jon Frazer. You look like the proverbial cat, you know." She leaned back to take more of him into view.

Jon dramatically played the offended one. "Me? Secrets?" He settled back against the cushions, grinning from ear to ear. "I don't know what you're talking about, secrets. I'm as open as they come." He shook his head. "Nope. No secrets here." He closed his eyes, a man in charge and dismissed the whole subject.

Christy jabbed him in the ribs. "You're up to no good. It's written all over your face. You can't deny it!" She moved in closer, an idea struck and she began to taunt him with tickles. Rudi caught on fast and they all ended up in a mass of gasping and giggles on the floor with Rudi sitting on top of Jon in victory, as Christy rolled on the floor trying to pull herself together.

"It smells good in here. Any chance there's something I could eat?"

Rudi piped up. "Mom says we can't eat the feast until tomorrow."

"Well then, I guess I'll have to eat you!" Jon rolled her over to the floor and pretended to gobble her up like a big bad noisy wolf, tickling her into squeals of glee.

"Stop!" Rudi giggled. "Stop! I'm not the feast!" she gasped.

Jon gave her a reprieve, laughing as he sat back on his heels to take a breath himself. He ran a hand across his middle again. It grumbled in reply.

"Whoa. You really are hungry."

"Starved. I was so busy I forgot to eat."

"We haven't had dinner yet, either. Of course, the last thing I want to eat is what's in the kitchen." She sighed.

Jon's face lit up. "My mother used to say the same thing. She'd spend all day in the kitchen cooking before Thanksgiving or Christmas, then by the time it was done she said she'd smelled it so much, it had ruined her appetite." He relished the memory for a moment as he looked at Christy. "Funny thing is, she usually ate pie after that."

"We have pie!" Rudi offered. "We have three pies! Chocolate, Pecan, and Sweet Potato Pie," she nodded. "Because it wouldn't be Thanksgiving without Sweet Potato Pie."

Jon laughed as he reached out and tousled Rudi's hair. "I don't think sugar is going to satisfy my appetite tonight."

Rudi's face fell and Jon had compassion for her. "How about we have a different kind of pie?"

Rudi's eyes got big with question.

"Let's order a pizza and curl up and watch a movie together." Jon looked to Christy for her thoughts.

Christy winked at him. "That sounds like a plan to me. I'm pooped!"

Jon pulled out his phone to place the order. "Why don't you girls pick out the movie and I'll order us up an anchovy and double olive pizza." He licked his lips in mock anticipation just before both girls attacked and took control of his phone.

CHAPTER EIGHT

THANKSGIVING MORNING, Christy poured herself a cup of coffee before dawn and sat at the kitchen table. It was going to be a very busy day what with the usual Thanksgiving meal followed by the opening night of *Skyline Christmas*. Most of the food was ready to heat and they would enjoy their feast together with Jon and a few neighbors early in the day. That left plenty of time to prepare for the evening events. She stopped her mental checklist for a minute and wondered if Jon had friends and family he would rather spend the day with. She would have to make sure to ask him when he woke up. Then of course, Julia would meet her later with the necessary equipment to make hot chocolate for the crowds at the park. And Dicker was sure to be in the big middle of everything in the neighborhood.

The hardest part of the day would be keeping

Rudi contained until Santa showed up with the real live reindeer. Even though Rudi knew the "full" Santa story, she always got excited about seeing the reindeer. She considered it her personal job to bring them apples and carrots to eat right out of her hand. She had a special way with them, even Santa said so himself.

Jon wandered into the kitchen rubbing sleep out of his eyes. It made Christy's heart flutter to see him sleep-mussed and looking like heaven in the middle of her kitchen. She stood and nestled into him and pulled his scent into her nose, letting the warmth of his body envelope her.

"Morning." He mumbled into her ear.

Christy laughed softly and pulled back. "Somebody stayed up too late playing through the night." She stretched her neck up to reach for his lips.

"Mmm. You taste like cream."

She smiled and let him taste again. "There's coffee."

"Why would I want coffee when there's you?" He devoured her mouth, slowly, reminding her of his kisses in the night and how he'd tasted every inch of her body.

"Keep this up and the coffee can go cold for all I care." She nipped at his lower lip.

He sucked at hers.

"Rudi awake yet?"

Christy playfully pinched him in the rear. "No, but I can't be persuaded back to bed. It's the big day, Mister! We've got a huge day ahead of us!"

Jon pulled her against him, rubbed against her softness, and groaned his frustrations out loud.

She traced his lower lip with her fingertip. "I promise to make the night worth waiting for." She replaced her finger with her lips and made a soft sound, letting it travel across his lips.

He squeezed her tighter and grumbled. "Any chance we can make everyone go home early?"

Christy grinned, rubbed his nose with her own. "No chance of that." She placed one last kiss on his lips. "Besides, I can assure you, Rudi will be the last one to leave the reindeer. So that means we're there until the lights go out."

Jon aimed for the coffeepot and poured himself a dark cup before leaning back on the counter to pull a jolt of caffeine into his veins.

"Hey." Christy's voice took on an element of uncertainty. "I know it was presumptuous of me, but I assumed you would share Thanksgiving with Rudi and me."

Jon looked at her then, nodded.

"Is there anyone else you would like to be with? Family? Old friends?"

Jon reached for her then, pulled her into his chest. "Nope. Family is all far away." He pressed her head against his shoulder and ran a hand down her spine tenderly. "I suppose I could ask Bear to drop by. He's always on the loose during holidays." He chuckled. "But everyone already has plans, I'm sure."

"Who is Bear?" She ran a hand over his bare chest before looking up into his eyes. "Should I be afraid of him, being called bear and all?" She teased him.

Jon harrumphed. "No. He's just big. Probably more teddy bear than grizzly, though he doesn't seem to want to belong to anyone in particular."

Christy let her face question him.

"He doesn't stay with one person long enough to call it a relationship before moving on to the next woman."

"Oh. I see." Christy nodded and let her head fall back to his chest.

"He has good reason, I guess. Or, so he thinks."

"What's that?"

"He grew up with five older sisters. Five very frilly, bossy older sisters."

Christy smiled and leaned back to look up at him again. "I'm guessing they put him through the ringer?"

Jon shivered. "I can only imagine. He must've had to parade around in tiaras and those silly feather things for them. All I know is he avoids family like the plague. He only shows up with a woman in tow when he has to. Otherwise, he's the guy at the bar with the pickup lines."

Concern crossed Christy's face. "Do you think he'll be okay with Julia? She's having Thanksgiving dinner with us."

"We don't know if he'll come yet. And if he does, he's a grown man. He can figure it out, okay?"

Christy looked at his mouth, let her mind go back to his lips and followed the thought with a kiss. It caused a deep sound to emanate from Jon's chest.

"You're going to taunt me all day, aren't you?" He pulled away and rested his forehead against hers.

"Only as much as I possibly can." She grinned at him, smoothed away the pout from his lips before taking one last nip at him.

CHAPTER NINE

AFTER A RELAXED morning of parades on TV and food heating in the kitchen, the midday Christy and Rudi Thanksgiving Feast went off without a hitch. That is, according to Christy and Rudi. Jon had a different perspective. One that revolved around a very good friend and a woman who escaped him. Mainly, Bear and Julia.

In fact, Jon had spent a miserable time with Bear that afternoon setting up the surprise light display for the evening. Bear grumbled and complained about Julia and women in general. Jon thought it was hilarious that Julia did not want *anything* to do with Bear. That had never happened before as far back as Jon could remember. Women usually stuck to Bear. He was a heartbreaker, that one.

Then again, as he had said to Christy that

morning, Bear was a grown man. He could take care of himself.

Once the lights were set and Jon and Bear had a *reveal* plan, they took a tour together around the neighborhood one last time to check things out. Jon had received a weather warning message on his phone earlier stating that the area was under a Fire Weather Alert until six that evening when clouds would amble into their vicinity. A Fire Weather Alert wasn't good. With the dry conditions and late autumn leaves flying around everywhere, all it took was one faulty electrical cord for things to get messy. But all checked out just fine until they got to one light show meant to outdo all others. Dicker's.

From a safe distance, Jon looked on as Dicker grumbled around his property. He was testing cords and looking for something. His behavior clearly suggested something was wrong with his plan. Jon continued to watch and resisted speaking up. The last thing he wanted was to tangle with Dicker today.

"You know this guy gets written up in the local paper every year for his lights, right?"

Jon looked at Bear and sneered. "Of course he does."

"You didn't know that, did you?" Bear grinned back at him.

Jon just shook his head.

"Are we going to stand here and watch him all

afternoon or are we going to call the fire department?"

Jon sighed and resigned himself to do just that. As he reached for his phone, a familiar red truck turned into the neighborhood and headed directly towards them, parking in front of Dicker's house. A man-in-charge jumped down from the truck, leaving his team in place and greeted Dicker with a friendly salute.

Dicker fumed at the sight of him and threw his hands on his hips, preparing for battle.

"Slow down there, Mr. Dickerson," the man in uniform shouted for all to hear. "No need to get yourself all riled up before you hear me out, now." He stopped in front of Dicker and, though Jon couldn't hear the exact conversation, he could make out the substance of it by their body language. The fire official appeared to be a professional at setting peoples nerves at ease. Dicker deflated faster than he had been ruffled. The firefighter gave a hand signal to his team, and they all dismounted form the big truck to begin a systematic exam of Dicker's property.

Bear kicked at a rock on the sidewalk. "I like Christy." He turned to face Jon. "It's good to see you finally take a slice out of life for yourself, man."

"What's that supposed to mean?"

"You know as well as I do, you're always

about everyone else, never about yourself."

Jon rubbed his belly and guffawed in self-defense. "I do just fine by myself."

"Yes. For yourself. As in you. Single. Alone." Bear sneered. "I'm just saying it's good to see you let someone into your life." He took his hat off and beat it against his thigh before repositioning it on top of his head. "She looks good on you, Jon." He pulled the hat further down looking for the right fit. "And that's that," he nodded. "I think I'm going to head down to the park and see if I can help the ladies." He wiggled his eyebrows.

Jon laughed at him openly and slapped a hand on his shoulder. "You might have met the one that gets away, my friend." His face split into a wide grin. "She's not exactly wanting to sew your buttons on, if you know what I mean."

A storm crossed Bear's face. "Yeah. Well, we'll just see what the score is at the end of the day, man." And with that, he stomped off in the direction of the park, alone, looking to score the attention of a woman who wouldn't give him the time of day.

Jon's laughter followed in the wind.

JON FOUND RUDI in the driveway, filling up a wagon with carrots and apples she'd collected from the neighbors over the past week. Clearly, she was on reindeer duty and taking her job quite seriously. He checked his phone for the time. They had about a half hour before the sun would slip below the horizon. Rudi would need a hand if she was going to get to the park and back before the lights came on.

"Need a hand with that?"

Rudi looked up, relief washed over her. "I thought I could handle it by myself but I can't get it to budge."

Jon reached a hand out and ruffled her short hair. "Maybe if we try it together we can get you there in one piece." Pride filled Jon as he watched the little girl work her mind.

"All right. But I don't want to let you do all the work. This is *my* project. Okay?"

Once the apples and carrots were delivered, Jon found Christy and corralled her, Julia, and Rudi back to 1224 Skyline Drive to prepare for the grand opening display of *Skyline Christmas*. Apparently, Bear had struck out with Julia once again because he was already stationed at Jon's house, ready to reveal the big surprise. He appeared to look much more like a grizzly than a teddy bear this go around though and his eyes seemed to follow one very uninterested woman. Surprise. Surprise.

Neighbors gathered around near Jon's house, waiting for his first annual light display. The fire truck still stood tall around the corner towards

Dicker's house within view of the entrance. Dicker himself stood under the *Skyline Christmas* banner that would begin the show. He wore a red and white fur hat. And with his oversized pocket watch in hand, he waited for the minutes to tick off before he queued the first of many lights to illuminate the night. Though tonight it seemed *old style,* tomorrow night they would all be on timers, in sync with one another such that the lights would come on all at once.

Dicker hadn't said a word about Jon's personal lawn decoration since he saw Bear and Jon position it on the lawn that morning. Of course, it was covered with a tarp until minutes ago. Soon, Bear would lift it back to anchor it to the ground and plug in the last chord to make it shine in the night.

Jon turned Christy to face her own house when the time came to turn the lights on. "You should get the first peek at your own lights, right?" He whispered in her ear. Rudi jumped around them, counting off the seconds with Julia.

Christy shivered with Jon holding her from behind. "I don't think the weatherman got it right tonight." She rubbed her gloved hands over her arms. She looked up into the night. "I don't see a star in the sky."

"I still say it's going to snow, momma!" Rudi piped in between counting down the time out loud.

Jon laughed. "Y'all keep saying that and

maybe it will."

And then Dicker shouted through his megaphone. . . "Three. Two. One." And the lights came on, over his head the banner shone as a bright welcome to all who entered, followed by the lights of the first few houses, one at a time, alternating. In order, Christy connected the plug of her own lights before they twinkled back at her.

She smiled. Rudi and Julia cheered. Jon slipped his hands over Christy's eyes and turned her to look at his house.

"What's this?" She covered his hands with her own and giggled. "Are you afraid they won't come on?"

A deep sound resonated out of Jon's chest. "No. They'll come on. I just want you to see them all in one look."

And then he moved his hands away so that she could see. There across the street, his home lit up, simple and grand with its white lights and fresh green wreaths and red ribbons all around. The candles shone out through the old windows and the little garden gnome smiled back at her in his twinkle-light-snow covered feet. Christy saw Bear make one last connection before she heard a collective gasp among her neighbors. Because there in front of her eyes was a wood cutout of a double heart that was bigger than Bear, outlined in white twinkling lights and covered in silver tinsel. But the biggest detail of all were the big red lights that read, *Be Mine!*

Christy gasped. Rudi squealed. Julia sighed. Bear stood stalwart. The neighbors all waited for her answer.

Christy covered her mouth with her hands as tears ran down her face. She sniffled as Jon eased around in front of her to see her face. Emotions ran the gamut across her face, questioning him.

He searched her eyes for a hint of an answer. "Will you? Be mine?"

"I don't understand?"

Jon wiped away a tear as he smoothed her face with his big hand. "I've looked for you my whole life Christy Layne. I want to keep you for myself." He searched her eyes, pulling at her. "So will you? Be mine?" Just then he remembered the extra sparkle and reached into his pocket to pull out a heart shaped diamond ring. He picked up her left hand and held it steady. "Christy Layne, will you be my wife by Valentine's Day?"

She looked all around her, her family of one and friends innumerable watching on. Even Dicker was smiling and waiting for her reply. And then she nodded. "Yes." Her head bobbed up and down. "Yes! I will be yours, Jon Frazer!" He scooped her up into his arms as electricity made its way down the street leading the cars to Santa and his reindeer." Rudi let out a big "Whoopee!" with her scarf sailing in the winds. "We're going to be a family!"

"Maybe now you can get some renovations done on your house." Christy teased him.

"It's not my house, sweetheart. It's ours. Our new home." His face stretched as wide as it could in joy. "We just got ourselves a renovated Christmas." He winked at her as the first of many snowflakes fell.

And they all traveled down the path to hot cocoa, Santa, and his reindeer.

ON VALENTINE'S DAY, Dicker placed an ad in the *Riverland News*. "House for Rent. Family needed. Christmas rules apply."

The End

Coming October 2014!

PAINTING SKYLINE
Skyline Mountain Book 2

Bear never cared much for being tied down until he found himself tracking Julia, the latest resident of Skyline Mountain. She's slipped through his hands on many occasions but Bear's made up his mind the time has come to put a stop to that.

Julia is enjoying her new home on the mountain and trying desperately to stay out of the line of fire from both her grandmother and a local bear. While her grandmother is about as under control as possible, Julia has made eye contact with the bear and he's not proving to be controllable.

With the help of his friends and family, Bear may be able to hold Julia still long enough for her to see his good side. Heck, he might even come out of hiding and shave for her! The question is, will Julia have anything to do with him once she finds out who he really is?

Here's a sneak peak . . .

"WHAT DID I do to piss you off now, Princess?" Bear stood there dripping pool water.

Julia gawked at him. He appeared to weigh mere ounces and made of air from the way he propelled himself out of Olympic sized pool with grace and efficiency. But he was. Well. *Ginormous.* And beautiful, if you liked the bigger-than-life-bear-like-appearance of a carefree, confident southern jock. She had a clogged pipe or something because air wasn't flowing in or out of her body.

He laughed. "I see you ignore my existence, yet again." He leaned down and grabbed a towel off the lounge chair nearest to him and began methodically drying himself without taking his eyes from her. "That's the way of it then. We'll just go on behaving as if I don't exist." He turned his back to her then and threw the towel over his shoulders before retrieving his shirt and keys. He slipped his feet into a pair of flip-flops, lifted his bike under arm, and moved toward the gate, her existence as invisible to him as she insisted he was to her.

Just as he waved a hand in the air, a salute to his final departure, Julia gathered herself enough to clear her throat. "That's not what I meant."

Bear stopped with his hand on the gate, listening.

"I mean" Julia squeaked. She adjusted the book and towel that were clutched to her chest before clearing her throat to finish. "You're not invisible."

Bear turned around with eyebrow raised, as if to ask, *did I hear you correctly*?

Her shoulders slumped. She sighed and let her head fall to the side lamenting the years of confidence training she'd worked through, but now stumbled to her feet in complete betrayal of her character.

Bear turned back around, fully facing her and closed the distance between them. He stopped close enough that she could feel the heat coming off of his body. He showed no emotion, but she could sense his intensity just the same. A muscle twitched on his jawline. His eyes softened. "What *did* you mean, Princess?"

Julia couldn't breathe. She could barely think a thought to completion what with him standing so close and looking her down as he was. "I um." She looked at his lips peeking through his overgrown beard. "That is to say." She turned her eyes towards the wall of the pool area that overlooked spectacular views of the surrounding fall painted mountains. "I don't." She shivered. It was seventy-eight degrees with no wind whatsoever. Her hands were cold and she shivered, again. He smelled of man and pool and sweat and heat. His skin glistened a warm brown proving his love of the outdoors. She looked down and noted his toenails were clean and tidy and white and neat. There was a white strip of skin peeking out from underneath his sandals. A fleck of periwinkle blue paint stuck to the "v" of his left shoe. *He must've worn them while working*, she thought. Julia closed her eyes and drew in a deep breath hoping for its cleansing powers. She exhaled slowly. When she opened her eyes and dared look back up into the face of the man who'd hunted her for months, she saw a smile gleaming back at her. A smile that was wide and generous and patiently waiting for her response.

Julia laughed at herself. "I'm sorry. I didn't mean to offend you. I didn't mean anything at all."

"So I'm to think you were just taken in by my god-like appearance and rendered speechless, is that right?"

Nailed it! She thought inside her head.

"But of course you couldn't say that because that would indicate that you noticed me and that's just not your style, is it Princess. Being royal and all. Right?"

Julia winced. "Please don't call me that."

"But isn't that what you are? A privileged young woman who has everything she could possibly want or need. Sounds like royalty to me."

Julia once again let her head fall to her chest and looked downward desperately trying to gain control of herself and maybe the situation. She bit her lip just as a large hand lifter her chin back up towards the sky.

"If you'd stop looking away maybe we could get past this little boxing match, sugar."

Julia couldn't help but follow the movement of his lips. Just as the word "sugar" left his mouth his tongue slipped out and licked his lips leaving a trail of unwelcomed provocative thoughts skipping across her mind. And still, she couldn't look away. *So what, she'd sworn off men. She could still look. There wasn't any harm in that.*

Bear's nostrils flared just enough to pull her eyes up a notch. A tree branch jostled behind her as a squirrel leapt from one tree to another. Bear's thumb reached up and smoothed across her lips. A dove cooed in the distance to her lover.

Julia's heart fluttered.

Bear's eyes dropped to half-mast and zeroed in on her mouth. "I think you're a royal pain." He then bent, reaching for their lips to collide.

Julia heard alarm bells ringing in the back of her mind but she squelched them and let herself be led to wherever he wanted to take her. His lips touched hers, lightly at first and then all she could think was how marvelous it was that his lips tasted like honey. Golden, delicious, liquid honey. Something sounded in the distance, a horn or maybe a whistle. She paid it no mind and made a noise of her own when Bear pulled the things from her arms and threw them behind her onto a chair. He slipped his hands back down to her sides and pulled her in tight against his big body. Her pulse ran fast and hard and now she was glistening with heat where less than five minutes ago she was cold as ice. A banging sound broke through the air as a car door slammed against its frame.

Julia jumped back and gave Bear a shove. A flush of embarrassment painted itself up her neck and all over her face before she could hide behind her hands.

Bear looked at the cover of the romance book he'd tossed out of her hands and let out a low growl in recognition of what the cover promised. Passion.

Confusion swept through Julia. She'd never in her life wanted to feel such strength and desire as that which Bear was dishing out but she knew she shouldn't encourage him. He'd been in pursuit for months now, always backing down when she told him no. But her body wasn't telling him no. It was screaming yes so loud inside of her she was certain he too could hear its screams of desire.

Bear pulled his arms across his chest and rocked back on his heels. "Well. Well. Well." He winked at her then and let a dimple peek out at her. "I think we've got ourselves a royal on the run."

Panic grew and escalated inside of Julia. Once again she couldn't speak, couldn't even think fast enough to respond before an arm slipped past her and she found herself once again within the paws of a bear, his lips so close she could feel the hair on his face tickle her as his lips moved.

"What are you afraid of, Julia?" His eyes bore down into her soul requiring her to cough up an answer. "Please put me out of my misery and tell me, what are you afraid of?"

She couldn't do it. She couldn't say a thing. His mouth moved to take hers into his control and she heard herself squeak. Squeak like a damn mouse terrified of the big badass lion, or bear as it were.

"I am not running the YMCA around here, Mr. Grecco!" Dicker stood a foot away from them, hands boldly on each hip, steam coming from his ears at a rate a large earth moving shovel would envy. In customary fashion, he sported loud plaid golf shorts, a screaming orange shirt, and a whistle around his neck in true self-appointed-Skyline-Mountain-lawman style. "Who on God's green earth gave you permission to come up on our mountain and use the pool facilities any time you feel the need to do so, sir?" Dicker turned and looked accusingly at Julia then. "And you! You haven't exactly been the poster child of conformity either, little missy! What gives you the right to break the rules and share this wealth with the likes of him?"

If there was anything, or rather *anyone*, who was enough to pull Julia back to her warrior self, it was Dicker. "Let me tell you something, Mr. Dickerson."

"Now, now, now." Dicker waved a finger in rejection to her salutation. "Miss Julia, you know I request that everyone call me Dicker. Not Dick. Not Mr. Dickerson. Just Dicker. It's the right thing to do here in the south where we all behave with impeccable, friendly hospitality." His mouth spread generously across his face almost making Julia believe he was being friendly.

"Dicker! Shush! You are a bully and a faker. Stop telling me what I can and cannot do. I won't have it. I pay my mortgage and my Home Owners Association dues just like the next guy and you have no right to tell me what to do. Besides, I wasn't using the pool for crying out loud! I came up here to enjoy the sunshine and I got accosted by a Grizzly!

Bear held an offended hand over his heart. "A Grizzly?" He let out a howl of laughter to the sun that made the tree branches sway and squirrels giggle in response. "You have *got* to be kidding me!"

Julia reached over and punched Bear in the arm.

"Hey!" He smoothed a hand over the offended arm. "What was that for?"

"You!" She pointed at Bear and huffed. "And you!" She swung around and pressed a finger into Dicker's face. "Men!" She exclaimed in frustration before bending to yank up her belongings and take off for the gate.

"What the hell was that?" Bear shouted in her wake. "You're not running scared, are you?"

Julia turned back to face Bear, and with all her twenty eight years of maturity and polish, shot him the finger. Then she stiffly turned back around, carried herself regally through the gate, and put as much distance as she could between them before her knees gave completely out from underneath her.

What she didn't hear in her wake was Bear sneering at Dicker.

"You have amazing timing old man."

"Maybe you're just not moving fast enough, Mr. Grizzly. Looks to me like you need some hibernation time to work out your strategy?" Dicker slapped at his knee reveling in his own delivery of fun.

Bear growled. "Yeah, well you need to mind your own beeswax, Dicker."

Dicker pulled himself tall as his body would stretch and aimed his finger up toward Bear's face. "Maybe so. But mark my words, Mr. Grecco. There's a bear on this mountain that needs to go swimming somewhere else. Fishing too, from what I just saw of Miss Julia punching you in the arm."

And with that, Dicker spun on his heels, opened the gate and ushered Bear to the street.

If you enjoyed reading Renovating Christmas, I would be grateful if you would help others enjoy this book, too.

Recommend it.

Please help other readers discover this book by recommending it to friends, reader groups, book clubs, and discussion boards.

Review it.

Please tell other readers why you liked this book by reviewing it on Amazon or Goodreads. And if you do review it, please contact me so I can thank you with a personal note or visit me at http://www.LesiaFlynn.com.

Lesia Flynn's Newsletter
is coming your way very soon!

You don't want to miss it!
Watch for details at Lesia Flynn's
various social media platforms so you too
can receive regular updates and participate
in giveaways and fun!

ABOUT THE AUTHOR

Lesia Flynn is a native of Louisiana. She studied graphic design at LA Tech University. She lives in northern Alabama with her husband, children, and a rescue cat named Chali2Na who is determined to save her from her daily goofball mishaps. She enjoys reading, writing, music and art, but most of all, anything that provides an adventure! Lesia loves hearing from fans.

Connect with Lesia Flynn online:

www.LesiaFlynn.com
facebook.com/pages/Lesia-Flynn
Twitter: @LesiaFlynn
Pinterest: Lesia Flynn

www.ingramcontent.com/pod-product-compliance
Lightning Source LLC
Chambersburg PA
CBHW020543130626
46552CB00007B/2736